Especially for Ali ! McKenzie ! Cannon
2002

Boo!

Wendy Watson

Clarion Books · New York

For Georgia and Rosey and Emily,
who helped with the words

Clarion Books
a Houghton Mifflin Company imprint
215 Park Avenue South, New York, NY 10003
Text and illustrations copyright © 1992 by Wendy Watson
Calligraphy on cover and title page by Paul Shaw.
All rights reserved.
For information about permission to reproduce selections from this book,
write to Permissions, Houghton Mifflin Company,
215 Park Avenue South, New York, NY 10003.

www.houghtonmifflinbooks.com

Printed in the U.S.A.

Library of Congress Cataloging-in-Publication Data

Watson, Wendy.
Boo! It's Halloween / by Wendy Watson.
p.   cm.
Summary: A family gets ready for Halloween, preparing costumes, making goodies for the school party,
and carving jack-o'-lanterns. Halloween jokes and rhymes are interspersed throughout the text.
ISBN 0-395 53628 6   PA ISBN 0-618-13057-8
[1. Halloween—Fiction.] I. Title.
PZ7.W332Bo   1992   91-43457
[E]—dc20   CIP   AC

BVG   10 9 8 7 6 5 4 3

Boo!
Watch out, everyone —
tonight is Halloween!

We're almost ready.
Mom is sewing our costumes as fast as she can.
Dad is showing us how to paint our masks.

Grandpa helps us carve jack-o-lanterns on the porch.
Leaves are falling everywhere.
We eat apples
and sing songs.

Inside the warm kitchen
we smell molasses and chocolate.
Grandma is making refreshments
for the party at school tonight.
We cut cookies and ice cupcakes.
Grandma stirs the baked beans.
Don't eat now, doggie—it's for the party!
But doggie doesn't wait.

It's getting dark…darker…darker…
it's time for HALLOWEEN!
We light the jack-o-lanterns.
We put on our costumes.
Grandma brings her makeup.
Mom finds safety pins.
At last we're dressed.
Let's go!

WHEN DO SPOOKS
USUALLY APPEAR?

RIGHT BEFORE SOMEONE
SCREAMS…

Look!
Now we *know* it's Halloween!
Here come witches and goblins, ghosts and ghouls,
pirates, monsters, skeletons, and spooks,
vampires and fairies,
hobos and princesses,
all going to the party.

The schoolhouse isn't a school anymore.
It's a haunted house.
Ooooooo o o o o o o o o o o .
Shall we go in?
Yes…but let's hold hands!

Thank goodness that's over!

Now we can eat.

Ghosts and skeletons get hungry, too.

And of course doggie is *always* hungry.

After supper,
we play games.

"Time for a scarey story," says Dad.
"Turn off the lights!"

EEEEEK!

A SCAREY STORY

Pompey was dead and laid in his grave,
Laid in his grave, laid in his grave,
Pompey was dead and laid in his grave,
Oh! Oh! Oh!

An apple tree grew over his head,
Over his head, over his head,
An apple tree grew over his head,
Oh! Oh! Oh!

The apples got ripe and started to fall,
Started to fall, started to fall,
The apples got ripe and started to fall,
Oh! Oh! Oh!

There came an old woman a-picking them up,
A-picking them up, a-picking them up,
There came an old woman a-picking them up,
Oh! Oh! Oh!

Pompey jumped up and gave her a thump,
Gave her a thump, gave her a thump,
Pompey jumped up and gave her a thump,
Oh! Oh! Oh!

It made the old woman go hipple-de-hop,
Hipple-de-hop, hipple-de-hop,
It made the old woman go hipple-de-hop,
Oh! OH! OH!

THE END

Quick—turn on the lights!

See? It's just us.

Now we can have the costume parade.

Who is the funniest?

Who is the scariest?

Who is the prettiest?

It's hard for the judges to decide.

Luckily there are lots of prizes.

HOW DOES A MONSTER COUNT TO TWENTY-THREE?

ON HIS FINGERS!

After the parade, the party is over—
but not Halloween!
The sky is dark.
The moon is full.
Ghosts howl behind every tree.
Now's the time for…

At last all the witches and goblins, ghosts and ghouls,
pirates, monsters, skeletons, and spooks,
vampires and fairies,
hobos and princesses
are tired.
It's time to go home.
Grandma and Grandpa and kitty are waiting.
Have a spooky Halloween,
everyone!